Dear Parent:
Your child's love of reading starts here.

Every child learns to read in a different way and at his or her own speed. Some go back and forth between reading levels and read favorite books again and again. Others read through each level in order. You can help your young reader improve and become more confident by encouraging his or her own interests and abilities. From books your child reads with you to the first books he or she reads alone, there are I Can Read Books for every stage of reading:

SHARED READING
Basic language, word repetition, and whimsical illustrations, ideal for sharing with your emergent reader

BEGINNING READING
Short sentences, familiar words, and simple concepts for children eager to read on their own

READING WITH HELP
Engaging stories, longer sentences, and language play for developing readers

READING ALONE
Complex plots, challenging vocabulary, and high-interest topics for the independent reader

ADVANCED READING
Short paragraphs, chapters, and exciting themes for the perfect bridge to chapter books

I Can Read Books have introduced children to the joy of reading since 1957. Featuring award-winning authors and illustrators and a fabulous cast of beloved characters, I Can Read Books set the standard for beginning readers.

A lifetime of discovery begins with the magical words "I Can Read!"

Visit www.icanread.com for information
on enriching your child's reading experience.

I Can Read Book® is a trademark of HarperCollins Publishers.

Alvin and the Chipmunks: Alvin Gets an A

Library of Congress catalog card number: 2012930218
ISBN 978-0-06-208603-7

Typography by Rick Farley
12 13 14 15 16   LP/WOR   10 9 8 7 6 5 4 3 2
❖
First Edition

ALVIN AND THE CHIPMUNKS™

Alvin Gets an A

By Kirsten Mayer

Illustrated by Jacqueline Rogers

HARPER

An Imprint of HarperCollinsPublishers

The Chipmunks just got back

from their concert tour.

Alvin, Simon, and Theodore

had fun singing for their fans.

Now they are home

and happy to go to school.

It is their first day back!

The Chipmunks say hi to their friends.
Alvin high-fives everyone
on the football team.
Simon waves to
his friends on the chess club.
Theodore greets everyone
in the cooking club.

"What class do we have first?"
asks Alvin.

Simon looks at the schedule.

"English class!" he says.

"Yippee!" squeals Alvin.

"Why are you so happy?" asks Theodore.

Alvin shrugs.

"Come on," says Simon.

The boys sit in their seats

while the teacher takes roll call.

"Alvin? Simon? Theodore?"

calls Mrs. Penny.

"Here!" the chipmunks shout.

"Class, you have homework,"

says Mrs. Penny.

"Write about your summer.

The report is due on Friday."

The chipmunks raise their hands.

"What *about* our summer?" asks Alvin.

"How long should it be?" asks Simon.

"Can we write about food?"

asks Theodore.

Mrs. Penny smiles.

"Write about what you did.

At least one page, please.

If you tried new foods, then yes."

"We were on tour together!"
cries Alvin at lunch.
"Why can't Simon write
one report for all of us?"

"I will not do your work.

Write your own report," says Simon.

"Can I have your cookies?"

asks Theodore.

After school,

Alvin sits down

to write his report.

He writes:

I went on tour.

I sang a lot of songs.

Alvin puts down his pencil.

He cannot think of anything else.

"Simon, help me," he says.

"I have writer's block."

"It is only one page," says Simon.

"You have lots to write about."

"But I want my report
to be special," says Alvin.
"Not the same as yours."

Next, Alvin asks Theodore for help.
"I am writing about the food
we ate in every city," says Theodore.
"Chili in Texas, ice cream in Ohio,
and corn on the cob in Kansas."

"Now I am hungry!" says Alvin.

"Let's make popcorn!"

"Okay," says Theodore.

Alvin goes to see Mrs. Penny.

"My report will be boring," he says.

"How do I make mine different?"

"What if you do not write the report?"
asks the teacher.

"Yay! No homework!" Alvin cheers.

"No, no." Mrs. Penny smiles.

"Give an oral report. Speak to the class."

Alvin goes home and thinks.

He gets out his guitar.

Listening outside his room,

Simon and Theodore hear lots of noise.

"Alvin! What is going on?" calls Simon.

"Homework!" yells Alvin.

It is Friday. Reports are due!

In English class

Simon hands in his neatly typed report.

It is two pages long!

Theodore hands in his report.

He pasted pictures of food on it

that he cut out of magazines.

"Very nice work, boys," says Mrs. Penny.

"Everyone, please sit down.

Alvin, will you share your report?"

asks the teacher.

Alvin goes up with his guitar.

Then he sings a new song he wrote

all about his summer!